the MONSTER DOCTOR

JOHN KELLY

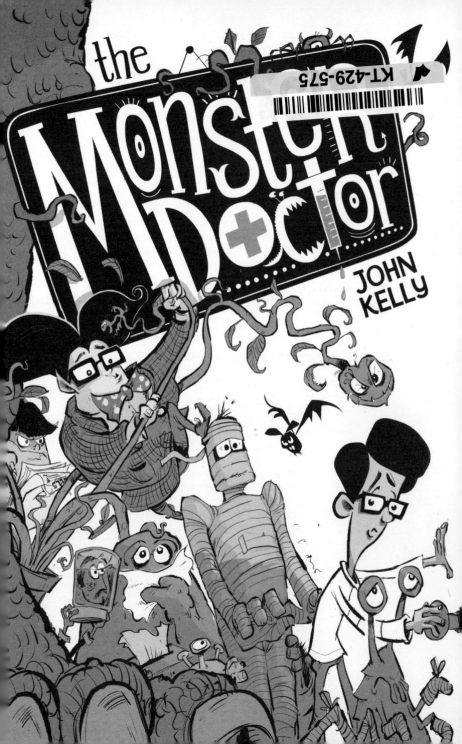

First published 2020 by Macmillan Children's Books
an imprint of Pan Macmillan
The Smithson, 6 Briset Street, London EC1M 5NR
Associated companies throughout the world
www.panmacmillan.com

ISBN 978-1-5290-2135-6

1 3 5 7 9 8 6 4 2

A CIP catalogue record for this book is available from the British Library.

Printed and bound by CPI Group (UK) Ltd, Croydon CR0 4YY

To my Mum, and Dad.

I wish Dad could have seen this.

CONTENTS:

COMPLETELY 'ARMLESS

Chapter 1

I was walking down the street one morning when the man in front of me **dropped his left arm** on the pavement.

Now, I don't know about you – maybe where you live people are **always** dropping limbs on the ground in front of you.

shuffle

shuffle

Who knows, maybe you can't walk to the shops without tripping over a **leg** or an **ear** or a **chin,** but, I can assure you, that's not the kind of thing you see every day around here. Oh no! Around here people drop normal things, like pens, bus passes or ice creams.

Not an **arm.**

But there it was, on the pavement at my feet.

A complete left arm.

The man who'd dropped it was just walking away. He was pretty scruffy, but that's no excuse to go dropping arms all over the place, is it? For one thing, the council will probably fine you for **littering.**

(Do body parts count as litter? I don't know. But I wouldn't google that if I were you.)

Anyway, I'm quite a helpful person (and not very **squeamish)** so I picked up the arm and went after him. I resisted the temptation to wave at him with it – that would have been **rude.** Luckily, the man hadn't got too far. In fact, he was shuffling so slowly down the pavement that catching up to him was really easy.

I tapped him on the shoulder. **'Excuse me,'** I said, **'but I think you've dropped something!'**

He stopped dead in his tracks and turned to face me. I was right about him being scruffy. He looked as if he hadn't had a bath in a year or two and **several of his teeth were missing.**

Then I noticed that his teeth (and his arm) weren't the only things missing.

Somehow he had managed to lose one of his **ears** as well.

And an **eye.**

And quite a big chunk of his **nose.**

'Hello, young man,' he said with a smile. 'Can I help you?' He seemed very friendly – though he was well overdue for a trip to the dentist.

I held out the left arm he'd dropped. 'I think this belongs to you,' I said.

He looked confused for a moment as he counted all the arms in front of him. There were **three** (which was one more than there really should have been). The penny dropped and he noticed his own arm was missing.

'Silly me!' he said.

'It's dropped off again, has it? I'm getting so careless these days. But how kind of you.'

He held out his remaining right hand in greeting.

'Morty Mort, at your service. Please allow me to shake your hand, young man.'

He shook my hand.

'Ozzy,' I said, shaking it back vigorously. 'Which is short for –'

His right arm came off in my hand.

I now had **four** arms.

Morty had **none.**

'If you don't mind me asking,' I said, 'are you ill? I'm no expert, but surely it's **not normal** for people's arms to just keep dropping off? Shouldn't you be going to the doctor?'

'Well, it's **funny** you should mention that,' he said. 'I was just on my way there when . . .' He looked down at his arms – the arms I was holding. 'Ah!' he said. 'That's going to be a bit **awkward.** The doctor's bound to need those to sew them back on, but I can't see how I can carry them like this.' He shrugged his armless shoulders.

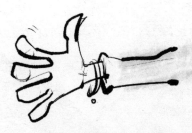

'Is it far to the doctor's?' I asked. I wasn't busy and, as I mentioned, I am quite helpful by nature.

'Why no! The surgery is just round the corner in Lovecraft Avenue. Not far at all.'

'That's odd. I've lived here for years, but I've never heard of Lovecraft Avenue.'

'Well, it is a **bit tricky** to find the first time, but if you'll do me a favour and carry my arms to

the surgery – if you're not too busy that is . . . ?'

I shook my head and he smiled that **gap-toothed smile** again. 'Follow me, then, and I'll show you the way,' he said.

I tucked his arms under mine. 'Do you mind me asking what's **wrong** with you?' I said as we walked.

'Oh, it's nothing serious,' he said, smiling. **'I'm just a little bit dead.'**

'Ah!' I said. Which was pretty much all I could think of to say. I've always suspected that there are **dead people** among us. For instance, rumour has it that Miss Longwhistle, the school secretary, hasn't moved her facial muscles in seventeen years.

Mr Gubbins in our street looks a lot like he's been **dug up** fairly recently.

But **Morty** was definitely the very first person I'd ever met to admit it to me.

9

LOVECRAFT AVENUE

Chapter 2

Now at this point most people would be thinking, *TURN ROUND AND RUN AS FAST AS YOU CAN!* So this is probably a good moment to explain that the reason I didn't is because of my family.

You see, my family are a bit odd.

For a start my parents named me **Ozzy,** which is short for – well, never mind that now. But the point is my family does things that other families don't seem to. Like instead of two weeks on a sunny beach we go camping in **Wales,** in the rain, while wearing shorts.

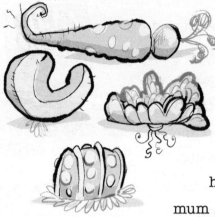

We don't get takeaway pizza. Instead we cook **strange vegetables** no one else has ever even heard of. Oh, and my mum and dad are very big on helping complete strangers – even when no one else is watching.

For example, that morning was the first day of the **summer holidays** and Dad had told me to, 'Find something useful to do with yourself. Join an anti-littering club, volunteer to comb *old ladies' beards* or even –' INSERT **SCARY MUSIC** HERE – 'get a job. It'll be character building.' He said this with a completely **straight face.**

BEARDS COMBED 50p

Mum had then pitched in and warned me that I was not going to 'Spend all summer in your room playing **RAPID RABID RABBIT RACING,**  eating bacon crunchies and making dreadful smells'.

Both excellent reasons to get out of the house.

On top of that, my **baby sister** is not yet two years old and is therefore completely, perfectly **horrible.** My parents, and everyone else, think she is just completely, perfectly *adorable*. But I'm not falling for that. After all, who knows what's normal behaviour for a toddler? One day I might walk into the living room and find her **eating** the **cat, breathing fire** or **sprouting insect legs**

out of the top of her head! So, compared to her, carrying a **zombie's** arms to the doctor's would be easy.

And, as a bonus, I'd be helping someone! Dad would be delighted. (Though I suspect he hadn't been thinking of **zombies** when he'd suggested it.)

As we walked, I asked Morty, 'Isn't it a bit of a pain being **dead?**'

He shrugged. Which was really the only gesture he could make, what with me carrying both his arms.

'Well, I was a **bit miffed** when it first happened,' he said, 'but, to be honest, you can get used to most things, can't you? Apart from bagpipes, that is,' he added quickly. 'On the plus side, at least I don't get ill any more.'

'So why were you on your way to the **doctor's**, then?' I asked.

'Oh, just to get these **STITCHED** back on,' he said, and he made a funny gesture with his head. I realized he was trying to point at his coat pocket. 'Would you mind?' he said. 'Left-hand coat pocket.'

I put my hand in there and pulled

 out three small objects. One was an **ear,** the other an **eyeball** and

the third was the **bobbly bit** missing from the end of his **nose.**

'The doc will fix these in a jiffy,' he said. 'She does a *beautifully neat cross-stitch*. Take a look at my neck! Go on!' He stuck it out like a chicken and, slightly nervous, I pulled his shirt collar to one side. There was a line of very neat stitching running all the way round his neck.

'My head fell off last week when I was playing **ZOMBIE FOOTBALL** in the park.' He smiled. 'Everyone in my team – **DEAD ROVERS** – fell about **laughing.**

Funniest thing **EVER!'**

'Don't tell the doc, though,' he added in a whisper. 'I told her I did it while I was changing the smoke alarm.'

We stopped by a rather ramshackle-looking building.

'And here we are!' he announced. **'The surgery.'**

It was a detached, **tall** and very **wobbly-looking** building somewhere between four and eight storeys high. It had dozens of windows, but none of them matched. Some parts looked as if they'd fallen down in the past and been put back up again, but in completely the wrong place, or uʍop ǝpᴉsdn.

'Watch out!' said Morty, and nudged me to the right with his shoulder.

CRASH! A **huge** lump of wall the size of a microwave landed where I'd been standing a second before.

'**Yikes!**' I said. 'The building's **falling down!**'

'I know,' said Morty. 'Terrible shame, isn't it? No money, you see. **ANNIE** is ever such a brilliant doctor, but the poor creature's got no interest in money. Always thinking about others. "You're a soft touch, Annie!" I tell her all the time. She doesn't listen to me, of course. But then **I'm dead,** so what do I know?'

There was a brass plaque that needed a polish beside the front door. It read:

10 Lovecraft Avenue
Annie von Sichertall VIII
M.D.F.R.S.C.D.
Fully qualified monster physician & surgeon
Anything treated
(No biting allowed within these premises)

'Blimey! Is that the time?' said Morty. He was looking at his own watch, which was upside down on his wrist – the one tucked under my arm. 'It's two minutes to nine. I'll be late for my appointment. Wouldn't want **DELORES** to be cross with me.'

'Is it safe to go in?' I asked, but, by way of
reply, he just nudged me slightly to the left. A
roof tile **smashed** into the ground where I'd just
been standing.

'Probably safer than staying outside,' he said.

I opened the door (Morty being a bit rubbish at
the whole door-opening thing) and stepped inside.

Morty headed straight for the receptionist's window, where a bored-looking lady was sitting behind a glass partition. She was watching TV on her phone. With another tentacle, she was flicking through a magazine called *SCARY STYLE*.

Hold on, you're thinking. Did he just say **tentacle?**

YES. I did.

In fact, Delores had **lots** of **tentacles!** As well as the **two** that were holding her phone and magazine, she was busy filing paperwork with a **third!** Numbers **four** and **five** were putting paper in the printer and refilling the coffee machine, while **six** and **seven** were knitting a tiny jumper with lots of even tinier sleeves.

Delores slid the glass partition open with tentacle number **eight.**

'Morning, Morty,' she said without looking up.

'Morning, Delores,' said Morty, smiling his best gappy smile. 'You're looking –' he searched for an adjective – **'busy** today.'

She carried on watching her soap opera.

Morty sighed. 'I've got a nine o'clock appointment to have my stitches put back in,' he said. 'Though it might take a little bit longer than I'd planned on account of . . .' He looked over to where I was carrying his arms.

'You'll have to wait, Morty,' Delores said, and pointed a tentacle towards the door marked **Doctor.** It was shut, with the muffled noise of raised voices coming from behind it. One of them was as deep as an **elephant** playing the double bass in an underground cavern.

'It's the nurse,' Delores explained. 'He's not a happy bunny. I mean none of us have been paid for three months, but **Yorrik** has had enough. He's always been a sensitive soul. And I'd have quit myself – if I wasn't such a people person,' she said, before closing the glass partition and going back to her TV programme.

Morty and I sat down to wait. The only other occupants of the waiting room were a small man and his daughter, and neither looked like monsters at all . . . though there was something **unusual** about the little girl, but I couldn't quite put my finger on it.

The man saw me looking at her and smiled.

'Kids, eh?' He laughed. 'The scrapes they get into!'

The little girl protested. 'That's not fair, Dad! Janice Dreambottle dared me to do it.'

I suddenly realized what was wrong. Her head was on **back to front!**

'Janice can turn her head all the way round,' she complained. 'So I had to show her I could too!'

'Well, **more fool you** for copying her,' the father scolded. 'Janice's mum is part owl, so obviously—' He was interrupted by the argument in the doctor's office.

It was getting **louder** and **louder.** Suddenly there was a **CRASH!** the sound of scuttling and scrabbling along the floor and then the **'THUMP! THUMP! THUMP!'** of something **very heavy** heading for the door.

What on earth is going on in there?

I got my answer a second later when the door to the doctor's office

EXPLODED

off its hinges.

HE SEEMED FURRY ANGRY

Chapter 3

For a second the whole doorway was filled with **dirty-white fur**, until someone managed to squeeze through it. Some*thing* would probably be more accurate. It definitely wasn't human. It had an enormous **furry snout** with nostrils the size of two ship's funnels, red eyes that had recently been crying and a mouth that opened very wide to show a set of chunky teeth as big as piano keys.

It was a **yeti,** and it was very **upset.**

'**THAT'S IT, DELORES!**' it boomed with a voice that was probably causing hideous ornaments to fall off mantelpieces in nearby houses. **I'M DONE!** It's bad enough she treats me like a **SLAVE!**

it moaned. 'But to **NEVER GET PAID!** I should have **DANGER MONEY** for working here! What did we do last Thursday? Went **TRAMPING** through the **BOG** to treat that **DEPRESSED TROLL!** Now I've got **ATHLETE'S FOOT** and you know **PERFECTLY WELL** that I suffer with my bad feet.' He lifted up what was the **biggest foot** I had ever seen, with the longest toenails I had ever seen too. 'Healing sick monsters is all very **NOBLE** and what-not, but **I NEED TO GET PAID** every now and then! **I'VE HAD ENOUGH.** I'm back off to work at the ski lift – if they'll have me after the avalanche last year.'

The yeti turned towards the front door and saw Morty and me sitting there, gawping. **'OH!'** it said, one huge, hairy hand going to its mouth, embarrassed. 'I didn't see you there.

Where are my manners? You must think me such an **AWFUL** monster, bellowing like that.'

'Not at all,' I said.

'You're *VERY KIND,*' boomed the huge creature, before turning back to the reception window. *'BYE, DELORES! I'M SURE I'LL SEE YOU AROUND.'*
Then it limped to the front door, squished through and disappeared. It left a very strong smell of damp dog behind.

'Was that yeti limping?' I asked Morty.

''Fraid so.' Morty shook his head. 'All yetis suffer terribly with their feet. It's the shoes, you see. They just can't get 'em big enough any more. Yorrik's the third assistant the doc's lost this year.' He sighed. 'I've told her she shouldn't be so hard on them. But she's never been able to find a nurse she was happy with since *Zaggadath* left to go and train at the **Monster Doctor Academy.**
Zaggy was such a nice monster. So good with kids.'

ZAGGY

29

Through the partially open door I could hear the distinct sound of something being chased around the room. 'Come here, you **LITTLE...**' and, 'Oh! You slippery devil! Get out from underneath that guillotine! Out! Out, I say! Don't make me come and get you!' Then suddenly the voice barked,

Will somebody please SHUT THAT DOOR?

Delores swept back her glass partition **angrily.**

SHUT IT YOURSELF!

she yelled with a voice like a **foghorn** trying to hail a trawler far out at sea. She **slammed** the glass partition closed again.

> **Do I have to do *everything* myself?**

the voice cried angrily from inside the doctor's office, and a hand grabbed the door handle from inside and yanked it **violently** shut. The door stayed that way for about three whole seconds before it crashed to the floor.

'**CALL BERT THE BUILDER!**' yelled the angry voice from within.

Delores opened her window again. '**BERT WON'T COME BACK UNTIL YOU PAY HIS LAST TWELVE BILLS!**' she roared, but, before she could close her partition, the unseen doctor bellowed back.

'**THEN MAKE YOURSELF USEFUL, AND SEND THE NEXT PAYING PATIENT IN!**'

This kind of thing was all obviously completely normal for Delores. She turned to the man and his backward-facing daughter. 'The **doctor** will see you now, Mr Beaty,' she said in a posh receptionist voice.

But the man stayed sitting down. I couldn't blame him – I wouldn't have been itching to go in either.

'Oh, after you, **Mr Mort,**' he said to Morty. 'I reckon your need is greater than ours.'

'Cheers, Bill! Very kind of you,' said **Morty,** and he hurried through the door. I followed behind, carrying his arms.

'**CATCH THAT!**' yelled a voice from my left. I spun just in time to see something come flying towards me. It was pink, **slimy** and looked like an extremely annoyed **rubber glove.**

It was heading straight for my face and each one of its little fingers was **wriggling** frantically like a **worm.**

I'm not that good at sports, but we once had a budgie called **Papillon** who didn't ever want to go back in his cage, so I do have some experience in catching **flying creatures.** I plucked the pink thing out of the air without even thinking about it.

'Oh, good catch!' yelled a figure climbing out from behind a very large filing cabinet on the far side of the room. The woman was wearing a horsey-looking tweed jacket and skirt, and clutching a large half-empty glass jar, **sloshing** pink liquid all over the floor.

This must be the **monster doctor.**

She was about five feet tall and had the same basic shape as a **cannonball.** Her arms were as big as a **gorilla's,** but ended in small and *delicate* hands. The top of her head was as pointy as a missile's nose-cone and crowned with the most amazing hairstyle I'd ever seen. I reckon the only way you could possibly get hair like that would be to paint the top of your head with superglue and stick an entire **horse's tail** to the right-hand side of your skull. Then you'd have to go and find another **horse's tail** for the left side.

'**DON'T JUST STAND THERE!**' she yelled, jumping up on to a nearby table. It was **jam-packed** with jars containing **unidentifiable** things (some looked very alive).

She **raced** along the top of the table, one arm outstretched and holding a *butterfly* net.

'THE OTHER ONE'S HEADING FOR THE DOOR!' she yelled. 'Don't let it get away!'

I made a grab for another *pink* **flying** thing, but the rubbery blighter bit me and headed for a nearby medical-waste bin.

'OW!' I said.

'Don't be such a **BABY!'** shouted the doctor. 'And don't let it get under there! It'll probably catch Gabble's Disease and be **dead** by the end of the week.

Or is that the one that makes them turn blue? I really should look that up!'

Trying to be helpful, I kicked the waste bin very hard. The pink thing skittered out and made a break for the doorway, but Morty stopped it neatly with his foot.

'May I introduce,' he said, nodding at the strange figure jumping down from the table and straightening her jacket, **'Annie von Sichertall.'**

'The Eighth,' said the doctor.

'Better known as . . .' he continued.

'The monster doctor,' I said.

YOU'RE NOT GETTING ANY LESS DEAD

Chapter 4

A few minutes later, Morty and I were sitting in front of the doctor's desk. We were watching her stuffing the last of the **rubber-glove creatures** back into its jar. Her huge blue-lensed spectacles turned in my direction. She seemed to look at me properly for the first time and did a double-take.

'Good gracious me!' she said, lifting her glasses for a closer examination. Behind them her eyes were green (with traces of purple and yellow). 'You are **perfectly ordinary!**'

How on earth do you answer that?

'Well, compared to what I've seen today,' I said,

'I would say I'm **VERY ordinary.**'

'What on earth were you thinking, Morty?' the doctor said with a **pained** expression. (She was either annoyed or suffering from indigestion.) 'Bringing an **ordinary** into the surgery?'

She was right. I definitely wasn't **unusual** enough for this place. I began heading towards the door – or at least the place where the door used to be – but Morty called me back.

'You stay right where you are, Ozzy,' said Morty. He turned back to the doctor. 'And don't you be like that, Annie. Ozzy's not your **ordinary** everyday ordinary. He gave me a hand when my arms dropped off.' Morty smiled that **big gappy grin.** 'Hand! Geddit?'

'I see being dead hasn't improved your sense of humour, Morty,' said the **monster doctor,** scratching an ear that was definitely far too pointy to be human, but not pointy enough for anyone to make a big fuss about it.

'What on earth **are** those things?' I asked.

She pushed the jar across the desk towards me. 'These, young **ordinary** person, are the finest **bile leeches** known to medicine. I reared them

myself from leech spawn.' She held another jar up
to her face and *kissed* the glass affectionately.
'Who's a lovely leech, then?' she said. The thing in
the jar responded by trying to eat her face.

I peered into the jar at the creatures. They
immediately tried to **suck my face off**
through the glass.

'What do they do?' I said. 'Apart from try to
suck your face off, that is.'

'They eat **monster bile**,' she said.

'Monsters get very **grumpy** sometimes, then they start moaning. Of course, moaning leads to complaining, and everyone knows that complaining eventually leads to **antisocial behaviour.** Before you know it, they are stomping buildings flat, shaking double-decker buses in the street and posting rude comments on internet forums.

But if you pop one of these *lovelies* on their schnozzle and let it go:

SCHLOOOOOOOPPP! –' she made the same dreadful noise that Arthur Boatwangle makes when he is eating soup in the school canteen – 'bile all gone. No more unpleasantness. One **happy** monster.'

I was about to ask why the bile leeches had been flying around the room, but she beat me to it.

'Yorrik, my former assistant, was a little clumsy and dropped their jar. We were having a perfectly calm discussion about it when, for **some** reason, he just got up and quit.'

'Paying him a bit of money and a few *compliments* now and then might have helped, Annie,' said Morty.

'Pffff!' said the monster doctor. 'I don't understand this new-fangled obsession with compliments OR paying for things. Seems a **dreadful bore** to me. Anyway –' she jumped up from her chair, nearly knocking the jar of **bile leeches** to the floor again – 'what can I do for you today, Morty?'

Morty waggled his empty sleeve.

The doctor frowned. 'Ah! **Been in the wars again I see.**' She turned and pointed a chunky finger at me. 'You, **Mr Ordinary!** Be so good as to pick those up for me, would you?' Morty's arms were still lying on the floor where I'd dropped them. 'We'll need them in a minute.'

I spread out Morty's other missing bits on the doctor's desk as she grabbed a battered old leather medical kit. She rummaged around inside it and pulled out the **weirdest** needle I'd ever seen. It seemed to be straight, hooked and a spiral all at once, but I don't know how that's possible.

'You're not **squeamish**, are you?' she asked.

'Not at all,' I said proudly. 'I can clear up dog poo, cat sick and I can even stomach Dad's **awful** scrambled eggs.' Everyone knows that Dad's eggs are the most **disgusting** substance known to man.

cat-sick   parmesan   dog-poop   dad's scrambled eggs

WORLD DISGUSTING-NESS SCALE

The doctor looked very impressed by that and passed me one of Morty's arms. 'Hold his hand while I **STITCH** him up.' And with that she set to work. Her tiny hands became a blur as they stitched all Morty's missing bits back on, one by one. As she worked, she talked, and talked, and talked . . .

'All this gallivanting around has **really** got to stop, Morty,' she said. 'You've got to take this **being dead** thing more seriously – it's a widely recognized medical condition, you know. **Jolly** clever people have been **studying** it for centuries. And, anyway, it's not very sensible for a man in your condition to be climbing a ladder to fit a smoke alarm.'

Morty winked at me as the doctor stepped back to study her work.

'There!' she said. **'All done!'** Morty's arms, eye, ear and the end of his nose were all back where they were supposed to be. At least for the moment.

'What do I owe you, Doc?' asked Morty.

The doctor waved his question away, but Morty wasn't having it.

'C'mon, Doc! You got to take my money! How are you going to stay open if you don't charge us? I'm all right financially. I've still got my pension. The small print never said anything about the **undead,** did it?'

'Oh, all right. I know, I know. You can pay Delores on the way out.'

'Quite right too, Doc,' said Morty as he got up to leave. 'Come on, Ozzy. I'll show you the way back to the high street.'

I went to follow him, but the doctor reached across the desk and grabbed my arm.

'You go, Morty,' she said. 'I'm going to have a word with this *charming* person.'

'OK!' said my new zombie friend. 'See you around, Ozzy!' And with that he left. I was now all alone with the **monster doctor.** She leaned back in her chair and swivelled from side to side. As she did so, I noticed that one eye stayed focused on me even while the other glanced across to where the row of specimen jars sat on a table.

This was a bit **disconcerting.**

Finally she spoke. 'You're very intriguing, young **Mr Ordinary,** or shall I just call you **"Oddy"?'**

I was about to interrupt her to say, 'My name is actually —' when a thought struck me. No one ever calls me by my real name anyway. At home it's 'Ozzy'. At school it's either 'Thingy', 'Oi, You!' or 'Weirdo'.

It would be quite nice to be just **'Ordinary'** for a change. Especially when everyone else around me was so odd!

She smiled and said, 'You interest me. You don't panic easily, you're not **squeamish** and you're rather good with your hands. That is a very rare combination in **ordinaries** – and in **monsters** too, for that matter. On top of that, you are not as **hideous** to look at as most **ordinaries.** Are you sure there aren't any **monsters** in your family? Maybe your father's father's father was a **fiend?'**

I thought about it for a second.

'Well, my **baby sister** is two years old and lives mainly on **earthworms** and **dirt,'** I said, 'so I suppose she barely counts as **human.**

My **Uncle Nigel** has **very thick fur** on the palms of both his hands.

And my *Auntie Ingrid* is convinced that she can talk to her potted shrubs.'

'Hmm . . .' she said. 'Interesting, but probably not relevant. Though, in my professional opinion, you should probably keep an eye on Auntie Ingrid,' she added. Then her expression changed. She pursed her lips and, for the first time since I'd arrived, she looked lost for words. Shuffling slightly uncomfortably in her chair, she mumbled, 'I've got a teensy favour to ask you.'

'A favour?' I laughed. 'Me? What can I possibly do for you?'

'The thing is,' she declared, 'I'm short-handed. My nurse has left me in the **lurch,** and I can't possibly get a replacement from the agency until tomorrow. I've got lots and lots of patients to see today and, to make matters **worse,** I volunteered to man the **Emergency Monster Doctor** line today. I don't suppose you fancy –' she actually blushed – 'giving me a hand?'

'What, you mean **working** here? Like a . . .' I paused. 'A part-time job?'

'Yes, exactly like that,' she said. 'How would you like to be a **monster-doctor nurse** for a day?'

DOG DROOL AND JELLY

Chapter 5

Well, Mum and Dad had suggested I get a job, though I reckon they were thinking more along the lines of a paper round. I doubt helping a **crazy doctor stitch zombie body parts back together** was what they'd had in mind.

'What exactly would it involve?' I asked. It certainly sounded a lot more interesting, and probably wasn't as dangerous as combing old ladies' beards.

The doctor waved her hands dismissively. **'Oh, nothing too strenuous,'** she said. 'Showing patients in. Making tea. Handing me various things. Tidying up. A bit of filing. That sort of thing.'

I looked round at the broken door. 'Nothing . . .
dangerous, then?'

The doctor smiled. 'Of course not!' she said.
'The very idea.'

'But surely I'm not qualified?' I protested.

The doctor laughed. It was like a water buffalo
being tickled. *'Qualified?'* she said. 'You don't
think I'm **qualified**, do you?' She laughed again
(a bit too enthusiastically, if you ask me). 'Being
a **monster doctor** is one of those things you
need to learn by doing it – like bungee-jumping, or
sticking live electric cables up your nose. No, wait!
That's not a good example. **Ordinaries** don't do
that – do they? Anyway, you know what I mean.'
An *idea suddenly struck her. 'But books have
their place, I suppose.' She yanked open a desk
drawer, and began rummaging around inside it.
'Now, where did I put it . . . ?' she said, emptying
a collection of random things out on to her desk.
There was a *half-eaten*
apple covered in
fluff and purple
mould.

52

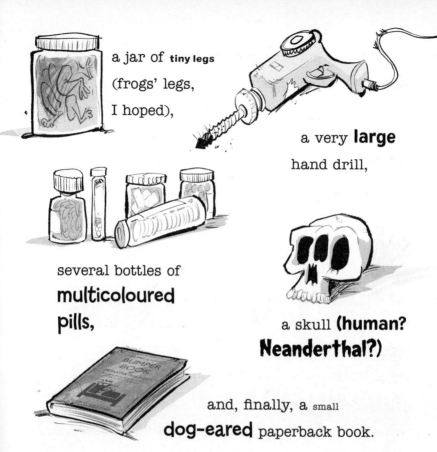

a jar of **tiny legs** (frogs' legs, I hoped),

a very **large** hand drill,

several bottles of **multicoloured pills,**

a skull **(human? Neanderthal?)**

and, finally, a small **dog-eared** paperback book.

'**AH-HA! Here it is!**' she cried triumphantly. 'I knew it was in there somewhere.' She gazed affectionately at the cover. 'I got this when I was very young, you know. Just before I left for the **Monster Doctor Academy.** I read it over and over.' She tossed it across the desk to me. 'Frankly, most of what you need to know to be a monster doctor is in there somewhere.'

It was very old (and smelt even older). It was bound in rough snot-green cardboard. There was a simple line drawing on the cover of a thing with **tentacles** looking poorly in an old-fashioned hospital bed. It had a thermometer in its mouth, and a bandage round its head.

The book was called:

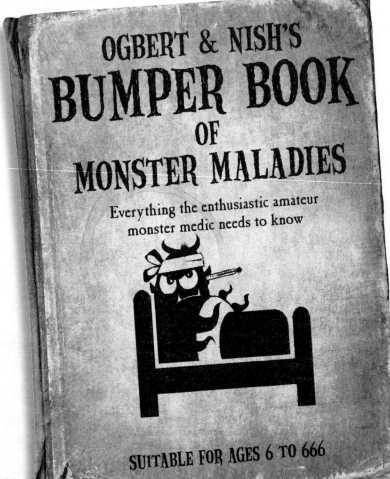

OGBERT & NISH'S
BUMPER BOOK
OF
MONSTER MALADIES

Everything the enthusiastic amateur monster medic needs to know

SUITABLE FOR AGES 6 TO 666

It was alphabetical, so I turned to the Ys.

YETI

Yeti fur has evolved for extremely cold environments. If yetis move to warmer climes for a new job or a long holiday, this can cause serious conditions such as sweaty yeti.

SYMPTONS:

Mild cases are identifiable by an overpowering smell of damp dog. More serious cases can be dangerous to any non-yetis in confined spaces. If the condition is not treated, sweaty yeti can become lethal to any non-yetis within a two-mile radius.

TREATMENT:

There is only one treatment: full body shaving. Medical professionals are advised to wear breathing equipment at all times when dealing with severe cases. This is best carried out at a properly qualified yeti-grooming parlour.

39

'So,' said the doctor, interrupting my reading. **'Shall we give it a go?'**

I nodded. She smiled broadly. 'Excellent! Then please show the next patient in, **Nurse Ordinary.'**

Back in reception I noticed that there was no sign of the man and his backward-facing daughter from earlier.

'Where'd they go?' I asked Delores.

Her glass partition was closed and there was a huge blob of something gooey sliding slowly down the glass. It looked like a cross between **dog drool** and jelly.

'The little girl went outside to play,' said Delores without taking her eyes off her phone screen. 'She got her head stuck in the railings in front of number fifty-three. Her dad pulled her out by her feet in the end. **Her head nearly came off.**' Delores smiled briefly at the thought of that. 'But at least it's the right way round now – or near enough anyway. The dad apologized for wasting my time.' She noticed I was still standing there. 'So, she's got you working for her now, has she?'

'I thought I'd help out for the day,' I said.

Delores looked me up and down briefly and rolled her eyes.

'That's what I thought back in 1837,' she said, and tapped on the glass with a **tentacle.** She was pointing over my shoulder. 'He's next,' she said. 'And he's made a **SHOCKING** mess in here. You can tell Annie from me that I am not going to be cleaning **that** up. Oh no!'

Someone sneezed very loudly behind me. **'A-A-A-A-A-AAAAAACHOOOOOOOOOOOO!'** Something splattered against the glass by my head. It was another **thick blob of icky** stuff.

I turned to see the creature responsible. It wasn't so much of a **creature** as a blob of transparent gel about the size of our **fridge-freezer** at home. On The Official World GLOOP Spectrum♈ he would have been towards the raspberry-jelly end.

The blob was sitting on – or around – one of the waiting-room chairs. You could see the seat through his **gloopy,** translucent body. There was a **HUGE** box of tissues on his lap (do blobs have laps?) and the floor around him was scattered with **gooey** used ones.

'I'm **tewwibwy sowwy,**' he said, and wiped his face. He didn't have anything I could call a nose. '**Bud I've god de mosht awfuw cowd.**'

The **normal** thing to do at this point would be to take one look at a creature like that and walk straight out of the door. But I'd already met a

dead bloke and a **yeti** this morning, so a snot-covered blob didn't really faze me. Besides, I was a trainee monster nurse now. There was probably some kind of professional standard to live up to. I smiled and gestured towards the doctor's door with my hand.

'Don't worry,' I said. 'The **doctor** will see you now.'

NOT A MONSTER AT ALL

Chapter 6

The snotty creature walked into the surgery. Actually, **walked** isn't really how he moved.

Imagine if you tipped a whole bucketful of **jelly** down the stairs.* Well, that weird flipping, slipping and flopping is how the snot creature moved. He **flol-lopped** into a chair – and then slowly **oozed** and flowed down around it.

'Come in – come in!' said the monster doctor. *'I don't believe we've met before. What's your name?'*

'Bob,' said the blob. **'Bob Blob.'**

---

* By the way, don't try this at home. It will ruin the stair carpet and – more importantly – is a complete waste of jelly.

'Any middle names?' asked the doctor, pen poised to make a note.

'**The**,' said Bob.

'OK, Bob. What seems to be the problem?'

'**A-A-A-A-ACHOOOOOOO!**' said Bob, by way of an answer, and a **bogey** the size of a cooking apple shot across the desk. It was heading straight for the doctor's face. She didn't flinch, but one hand moved impossibly fast and the bogey **SPLODGED** into it. The doctor calmly raised the hand to her face to examine the **gloop** better. It dripped from her fingers as she pulled out a Dictaphone and began to dictate notes into it.

'The patient is exuding as much snot as a Moldovian lung booger.'

She flicked some of it on to the blotter and watched it **quiver** for a moment. Then she continued to dictate.

'The consistency is halfway between the drool of a very large dog and **Gorgonzola-flavoured jelly.** Although it doesn't smell quite as pleasant as either.'

The doctor looked over at me. 'Nurse Ordinary, what does it say in the comprehensive medical literature about this?'

I realized she meant the book she'd just given me. I flicked through MONSTER MALADIES looking for the B section. **'Baba Yaga'**... **'Banshee'**... **'Basilisk'**... on and on through to **'Bogeyman'**... **'Bugbear'**... **'Bukavac'**...

There was no section on 'Blobs'.

'There's nothing in here about blobs,' I said. 'Nothing at all.'

The doctor smiled. 'That's because Mr Blob – sorry, **Bob**,' she corrected, 'is not a monster at all.'

I was confused. He looked a lot like a **monster** to me.

The doctor explained. 'Your first lesson is to understand the difference between **monsters** and **THINGS**,' she said. '**Bob** is a **THING** – no offence intended, **Bob**.'

Bob looked unconcerned. 'None taken,' he said, sniffing.

Monsters? THINGS? I was more confused. 'Aren't they the same?' I said.

'Not in the slightest,' said the doctor. '**Monsters** are simply creatures that have always existed: **vampires, werewolves, dragons, chimeras, teachers,** et cetera. All these are **monsters.** If monsters have a baby, it will always be a **monster** – or at least **part-monster.**'

That explained a lot about my school.

She pointed to Bob. '**THINGS,** on the other hand, are one-offs. They start out **ordinary** –

just like you – but get turned into **THINGS** by a **weird** and **VERY** rare event. Being bitten by a **radioactive** spider,

falling into a container full of **toxic waste,**

finding a **magic porcupine** in the forest called **Nigel** – that sort of thing.'

She turned to **Bob.** 'For instance, you weren't born this way, were you? How did you become a **blob?**'

Bob snuffled unhappily. **'Certainly not, Doctor.** I used to be a lifeguard. Lots of fresh air, sun, sea and swimming.' He looked down at where his tummy would have been once. **'I even had a six-pack!'** He sniffed. 'But then one day I was bitten by a **mutant jellyfish.** Some people get superpowers – lucky so-and-sos. **What do I get?'** He **wobbled** slightly, which I suppose was his best effort at a shrug. 'I get turned into a **blob!'**

He sniffed again. 'How am I supposed to be a **lifeguard** like this? You can't even see me in the water any more. I tried wearing a **bright red swimsuit,** but I just looked **ridiculous.**'

It was a pretty horrible thought.

'So now I'm **unemployed,**' said Bob. 'And, to make matters worse, I always seem to have this blooming cold – A-A-A-A-ACHOOOOOOO!'

The doctor dodged another blob of goo. It splattered against the wall behind her and ran down a poster *warning* about the dangers of eating human food. (At least I think that's what it said.)

'Let's not admit defeat too soon,' chided the doctor. 'There are lots of things we could try. For instance, if we freeze your—'

'Done that,' said **Bob**. 'I turned into a **giant snot-sicle.**'

'What about wearing a very thick blotting-paper mask?' suggested the doctor.

'Tried it. It just becomes snotty **papier-mâché,**' said Bob.

'I suppose we could try drying you out in a hot—'

'**Nope.** If I get too dry, bits of me start falling off,' said Bob.

'**Fascinating,**' said the doctor, rather unhelpfully. 'An intriguing problem. We'd better start with some tests, then.' She held a glass test tube out towards me. '**Nurse Ordinary,** please

take a sample of Bob's snot—' she began,
but Bob sneezed again.

'A-A-A-A-ACHOOOOOOO!'

This time the **bogey splattered** all over the jar
and the doctor's hand. She shook the excess goo
from her sleeve and handed me the (now full) jar.

'Put that somewhere safe, please,'
she said, and she reached for the
multicoloured pills I'd seen earlier.
She shook two from the bottle.
They were striped pink,
black and green. 'Take these.
They're **monster aspirin**

and should help you feel a little bit better. Now
return to the waiting room, please, and—'

I was about to say, 'But I thought you said
Bob was a **THING?** Surely a **THING** shouldn't be
taking **monster aspirin?**' But before I could
speak the doctor's phone began to ring. At the
same time a light on the wall began to **flash**
purple and green. Somewhere out in reception a
horrid **jangling bell** was ringing.

'What's happening?' I asked as the doctor pounced on the phone.

'M.D.E. line,' she barked, then began furiously making notes on a pad. **'Yes . . . yes . . . I understand. Absolutely. Right away!'** Then she slammed down the receiver, tore off the note, **sprang** to her feet, grabbed her coat and was suddenly over by the doorway (without touching the floor at any point).

She smiled calmly at Bob. 'If you wouldn't mind waiting, Bob, this call-out shouldn't take long.' Then she turned to me. **'Nurse Ordinary,** kindly show **Mr Blob** back to reception, then get your coat and my small case.' She pointed to a very large suitcase on wheels. It was big enough for a **two-week holiday** for a **family of four.** 'I'll meet you

out front with the **ambulance** in thirty seconds.'

'You've got an ambulance?' I said.

The doctor looked at me as if I was the strange one in the room.

'Of course I've got an ambulance,' she said. 'How on earth would we get to a monster emergency otherwise?'

WE GO BAT WAY

Chapter 7

Thirty seconds later the **monster ambulance** screeched to a halt in front of 10 Lovecraft Avenue. The **ambulance** was **massive!**

It had clearly once been a security truck, but it was now painted white(ish) with the same purple symbol stencilled on the sides, top and rear.

It was a bit like two
snakes/tentacles/wingy
things having a wrestle while
a single eyeball watched. I have
no idea what it all represented.

73

Something was written below it in several **strange languages.** The only one I recognized was **Latin,** and it read: 'CURIA OMNIA'. (I've since found out it means 'HEAL ANYTHING', which has been the motto of the monster doctors since the beginning of time.)

The ambulance, like everything else at the monster doctor's surgery, had seen better days.

From the state of its bodywork, it was clear it had (at some time or another):

1. been **crashed** a lot. Either that or it had fallen off a very **tall** cliff (it might have done both, I suppose);

2. spent some time at the bottom of a **sea** or **river** (this wasn't difficult to work out as there were still starfish and crab claws wedged behind the front bumper);

3. been on **fire**. It was **charred** (all over) and the left wing mirror had been melted into a blob (I didn't like to think about what might have caused that); and

4. most worrying of all, the ambulance had
   clearly been picked up by something with
   fingers (or **claws**) big enough to leave its
   marks in the roof.

The doctor yelled above the engine noise. **'SLING
THE CASE IN THE BACK AND GET IN!** Lance is
itching to get going.' She had a pile of cushions
under her bottom so she could reach the huge
wheel.

I jumped into the passenger seat, **slammed**
the door and we roared off down the road.

'Who's Lance?' I asked, looking around. But
there was no one else in the cab.

'Why *this* is **Lance,** of course!' she answered. 'You're sitting in him. **Lance** is the best **ambulance** I've ever had.' The doctor patted the steering wheel affectionately. 'You've seen me through many a scrape, haven't you, boy? **Who's a good boy?'**

She tickled the gear lever and Lance's engine revved, almost as if he was replying. I was about to ask if Lance was **alive** when I noticed an UNUSUAL ORNAMENT on the dashboard.

'**Doctor,**' I said, 'why have you got a **live bat** in a jar?'

'That's **BRUCE.**' She tutted, handing me a paper note. 'Don't tell me you've never seen a BAT-NAV before?' The note was the address she'd taken from the phone call. 'Just tell Bruce where we're going. He'll do the rest.'

The little bat chirped, flapped its wings inside the jar and the **LED** screen lit up. (I didn't mention that there was a small **LED** screen attached to the bat's jar, did I?)

These words **flashed** across it:

HURRY UP, DUMMY!
THIS IS AN EMERGENCY!

'There's no need to be **rude!**' I said, and I read out the *scribbled* note.

The bat squeaked again and the **LED** screen **flashed.**

> Carol's castle
> Mt Ignition
> little Flamington
> DR8 GON

IN 100 METRES TURN LIFT.

LIFT?

'We can't turn LEFT,' I said. But the bat in the jar (Bruce) flapped angrily and hissed.

The screen **flashed:**

I SAID, 'LIFT'!

'That doesn't mean anything,' I said.

The doctor just laughed. 'If Bruce says **LIFT,** then **Bruce** means **LIFT!**' And she pulled hard on the steering wheel. It telescoped back towards her chest.

Now, I'm not old enough to drive, but I'm fairly sure that steering wheels aren't meant to do that. And I'm also fairly sure that **security trucks** that have been turned into **ambulances** don't suddenly start spinning round and round and round like an **out-of-control carousel.** But this one did.

It turns out **Bruce** was right because we didn't go straight ahead, or right. In fact, we didn't go left or up or down either. We went sort of **corkscrewing** sideways while dropping, moving backwards and turning inside out. It was even more **unpleasant** than the school run when Dad is late and there are lots of speed bumps.

Then the view out of the window suddenly changed.

The railings, front gardens and recycling bins
of Lovecraft Avenue were gone. In their place
was spiky grass, **water buffaloes** and a man
wearing a straw hat shaped like a wok.

'**ARGH!** Where are we?' I asked. (I probably
screamed it, actually, but 'asked' sounds braver.)

'It looks like Vietnam to me,' said the doctor
casually. 'Somewhere near the town of **Hòa Bình,**
if I'm not mistaken.'

The bat **squeaked** again.

IN 50 METRES TAKE THE UNDO EXIT.

We were heading towards a very surprised-looking **water buffalo** when the doctor did something even stranger with the steering wheel. I'm not even going to try to describe what **'UNDO'** is (mainly because I don't understand), but let's just say that it wasn't much better than **'LIFT'**. When it finally stopped, I swallowed a little bit of **sick** and realized that the view had changed yet again.

'This may sound like a **stupid** question, but are we driving up the side of the **Eiffel Tower?**' I asked, knowing full well that we were.

'Only for a few seconds,' said the **doctor.**
Because right then the BAT-NAV was already
giving her his next instruction.

AT POINTY TOP PULL A REVERSE-WIBBLE.

So we did that. **'REVERSE-WIBBLE'** wasn't
very nice either. But at least when it was finished
we were clearly back on something that looked
like a road. In fact, it was quite a pleasant road. It
climbed **higher** and **higher** with every twisty turn
we took. And, even though there were dangerous-
looking cliffs on one side, the lack of water buffaloes
and Eiffel Towers made me like it even more.

'What on earth just happened?' I
whimpered, unclenching my hands and trying
to pull them from deep inside the stuffing of
the passenger seat. 'Where have we been and
– more importantly – why are we following the
directions of a **bat?'**

The doctor, who was rather busy not driving
the ambulance off a cliff, opened the glove box
(I'm sure I saw a tongue inside it) and tossed me
a small manual. 'Read this,' she said.

So I did.

Optional extras available for your monster ambulance ←

A. BAT-NAV

Although monster ambulances can travel anywhere in the six known dimensions, they're sadly a bit thick when it comes to knowing where they actually are. Luckily the STOKER BAT-NAV knows exactly where it is at all times. Simply tell the BAT-NAV where you want to go and it will tell your monster ambulance. All STOKER BAT-NAVs speak fluent Ambulance. Then just sit back and enjoy the ride.

B. SICK BAGS

C. FLAME-PROOF STEERING-WHEEL COVER

* Please note that due to a manufacturing fault all BAT-NAVs marked Bruce are extremely rude.

83

I looked up as we **scraped** round a corner and was aware that we were suddenly on top of the mountain. Up ahead was a **castle** shrouded in mist.

The dashboard **BAT-NAV** squeaked one last time.

CONTINUE FOR 500 METRES.
YOUR DESTINATION IS STRAIGHT AHEAD.
OBVIOUSLY.

Bruce wrapped his wings round his head and the screen went blank.

'So the **ambulance** is **alive?**' I said. But, before the doctor could answer, it made a noise like a cross between **revving** and purring. I patted the seat cautiously and said, *'Nice ambulance.'* Lance purred again.

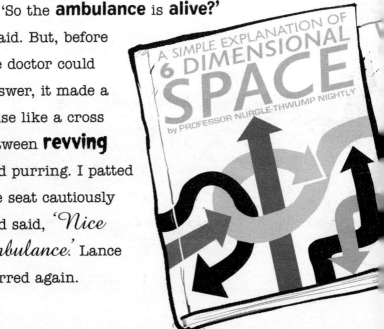

A SIMPLE EXPLANATION OF 6 DIMENSIONAL SPACE
by PROFESSOR NURGLE-THWUMP NIGHTLY

'Aw!' said the doctor. **'Lance** *likes you.'*

'So there are six dimensions, then?' I asked, changing the subject. **'Silly me.** I thought there were only three.'

The doctor shook her head sadly. 'Three dimensions? What on earth are they teaching you at school? No wonder you're always getting lost in supermarkets! Every **monster** child knows that there are six dimensions. But we can continue your education later. For now, you need to **concentrate.** *We have reached our patient.'*

She pointed through the windscreen to the CASTLE up ahead (presumably CAROL'S). Its twin towers stretched up into the **sky.** At ground level the place was wreathed in pale blue smoke that was lit up by the **flashing lights of a bright red fire engine.**

Phew! I thought. At least someone more **sensible** than us was here.

But as we drew closer one of the two towers began to bend like an **elephant's trunk.** It swooped down, grabbed the ladder off the top of the fire engine and ripped it free.

One of the firemen did an angry little dance, pulled out a megaphone and started **shouting** up at the bendy tower. I got the impression he wanted the bendy tower to leave his ladder alone.

'**Doctor,**' I said, 'did one of the towers on the castle just grab a **fireman's ladder,** or am I **hallucinating** after the journey?'

'That's no tower!' The doctor laughed. *That's our patient,* CAROL!' And as she said the name a **gigantic** pair of scalloped wings spread out from within the castle walls.

'Ah!' I said.

It wasn't a tower.

It was a DRAGON.

A really, really **big DRAGON** called CAROL.

OLD MISS JORGENSEN?

Chapter 8

'Y̶ou **INTERFERING**
nincompoops!' yelled Carol.
She was standing with her claws on her
hips, glaring down at the fireman. It was
exactly the same pose that my mum had
used when she'd found my **home zoo.***
My mum is pretty **scary** when she
does that. But **CAROL** had her beaten by

---

* (To be honest, I still can't see what the problem was with having two
rabbits, three guinea pigs, twelve assorted mice and a grumpy crab
called Neptune hidden underneath my bed.)

miles! Admittedly, Carol had the advantage of being **fifty feet tall** and covered in scales the size of hubcaps. She also had claws with scoops like a digger's, one of which she was currently pointing at the chief fireman.

'What on **EARTH** makes you think you can just **TURN UP** at someone's house and squirt **TEN THOUSAND GALLONS OF WATER** into their kitchen window?' she growled. 'And half of it went down my **THROAT!** And now look at the state of my **flame!**' Her mouth opened as wide as a car ferry getting ready for boarding, and she blew heavily on the fireman.

Nothing came out.

Well, no flames did anyway. There was a blast of **whiffy breath** and some damp blue smoke that smelt of cows and soggy paper. But that was it.

'**USELESS!**' sobbed Carol. 'What good is a dragon without fire? And it's all **YOUR FAULT.**'

For most people, having an **enormous dragon** yelling at them would be, at minimum, a bit worrying. But the chief fireman didn't seem bothered at all. (It probably helped that he was clearly a **monster** as well.)

'Madam,' he said quite calmly. 'We had a reliable report of a **dangerous chip-pan fire** from the lady who lives down there.' He pointed to a small cottage further down the hill where a little old lady with hooves, horns and big hair was pottering around in her front garden. She was busy raking leaves and pruning roses, seemingly totally oblivious to what was going on above her.

Carol's **huge** eyebrows raised like the opening of Tower Bridge.

'*Old Miss Jorgensen?*' she snorted, blue smoke puffing from her **huge** nostrils.

'Miss Jorgensen only moved in last week. I went round there with a moving-in gift. *"Hello!"* I said. "I'm your neighbour. You may notice that I'm an **enormous dragon.** So every now and then there's bound to be some smoke, a little **fire** and the occasional **roaring** from my castle. But don't you worry, *dearie.* Everything is fine, and here's a nice basket of *muffins."*

Old Miss Jorgensen nodded and smiled in all the right places. It was only later I found out she was – how shall I put this – hard of hearing and a **wee** bit short-sighted.'

The fireman shrugged. 'Well, I can see now that it's all been an **unfortunate misunderstanding,**' he said, and he jumped back into the fire engine. 'Very sorry to have troubled you, *madam*.' He waved to his fire crew. 'Pack up all the hoses! Back to the station for us – just in time for tea!'

'Oh, lovely!' said Carol. 'Super. Well, who's going to save the poor people of Pangolin? I'm supposed to be there by **midnight**. I have to burn the fleet of **Wodon Wulf-tree** and his wooden warriors. They're about to invade Pangolin Bay. I've been booked in for weeks! Can't you relight

Wodon Wulf-tree

my **fire**, or something?'

'I'm very sorry, ma'am,' said the chief fireman. 'But the **Monster Fire Service** takes fire safety very seriously. We can't just go around starting fires, now can we?' he said, and he drove away.

Carol sat down heavily on the ground, which shook as if we were in the middle of a small earthquake.

The monster doctor chose that moment to step forward. She held out her hand and said, 'Miss Carol? I'm from the **Emergency Monster Doctor** line.'

'Oh, thank heavens you're here,' she exclaimed.
'Just look what those **IDIOTS** have gone and done,' and with that she opened her **enormous jaws** alarmingly wide. When the pale blue smoke cleared, it was possible to see quite a lot further down her throat than I would have liked. Personally, I couldn't take my eyes off the **triple rows** of **razor-sharp teeth** in her mouth.

Each one was the size of a chef's knife.

The doctor peered in and tutted. 'Oh, dearie me! A very nasty case of dragon-damp.'

'I know. It's a **complete disaster,**' said Carol.

'Can't you just relight it?' I interrupted.

'Please forgive my young assistant,' said the doctor. 'He's just started today and,' she added in a half-whispered aside, 'he's **ordinary,** you know.'

Then she turned to me and said, 'Read the section on **Dragon damp** in ***Monster Maladies*** while I fetch some equipment from the ambulance.'

I pulled out the old book and thumbed through to the D section until I found this.

RISING DRAGON DAMP

Dragons who fall into rivers, spend too long in the rain or at the seaside can occasionally get rising dragon damp.

SYMPTOMS:

An excess of sparks, an unpleasant foggy blue smoke, and a weak flame. Extreme cases suffer the dreadful embarrassment of not being able to fly, burn enemies or melt solid gold.

TREATMENT:

Holiday somewhere nice and hot like Mexico or inside a volcano. Failing that, wear warm winter clothing (jumpers made from chainmail and human hair are highly recommended).

EMERGENCY TREATMENT:

Light a fire inside the dragon stomach. This is tricky*. It means crawling down the throat of a dragon, carrying hot coals or a flamethrower.

VERY DANGEROUS!

---

*Protective clothing should be worn whenever you are near (or inside) a dragon.

When I looked up, the monster doctor was shutting the back doors of the ambulance. There was a pile of gear on the ground: a long rope, a suit and helmet that looked like a beekeeper's outfit, two walkie-talkies and a large **blowtorch.**

Wow! I thought. *She's really going to do it! The monster doctor is actually going to crawl right down a dragon's throat and relight its fire.*

She beckoned me over.

'I'm going to need your help, nurse,' she said. 'I need you to—'

'I know! I know!' I said **excitedly.** 'I've just read all about it. You can depend on me.' I reached for what I assumed was the **safety rope.** 'You can count on me to pull you out.'

The monster doctor smiled.

'I don't need you to hold the rope,' she said, pointing at Carol. **'I need you to go in.'**

AN AWFUL WIND

Chapter 9

'**No way!**' I said. 'You told me I wouldn't have to do anything **dangerous!** But this is dangerous and stupid with a side order of suicidal.'

The doctor stepped forward, patting the air in that way people do to calm **frightened** animals.

'Possibly, very possibly,' she agreed. 'But the line between a **brilliant** idea and a **stupid** one can be extremely fine. Was *Nicholas Franjipan* mad when he invented **lunar-proof underwear for werewolves?**' she asked.

I had no idea and said so.

'Well, yes, he was, actually,' she admitted. **'Completely stark-staring bonkers,** as it happens. But that's not my point. My point was – what was my point again?'

'You want me to climb into an **enormous dragon's stomach,'** I reminded her.

'Ah! Yes! That was it,' she said. 'Now, to the uninformed, that may well seem an extremely dangerous thing to do. But I can assure you that it is not.'

I held out the battered copy of **Monster Maladies** to her. 'It says it is in here.'

She grabbed the book and flung it into a nearby shrub. 'Who gave you that **drivel?'** she said. 'I myself have carried out this procedure hundreds of times over the centuries and never received anything worse than **third-degree burns** over the lower half of my body.'

'Then why don't you do it?' I asked.

The doctor patted her thick waistline. 'An over-fondness for *chocolate-coated* sea urchins has left me a little less lithe than I used to be. I'm afraid to say that my days of tunnelling through a **dragon's gullet** are long gone. Anyway, that's why I have assistants!' She slapped me heartily on the shoulder. 'Someone **young** and **brave** and full of **derring-do!** And, most importantly, **slim.**'

And stupid, I thought.

The doctor was interrupted by an **explosive** belch. It was as loud as a clap of thunder – but much, much **smellier.** Carol had her claw to her snout and was looking embarrassed.

'Pardon me!' she said. 'I don't know what's wrong with me. I've suddenly got the most awful wind, and –' she belched again – 'it seems to be getting **worse!**'

'Oh dear,' said the doctor, suddenly looking very concerned. 'This is bad. What did you eat for lunch?'

Carol thought for a moment. *'Not much. A small hatchback car, a letterbox and a wagon full of logs pulled by four oxen. Just a snack, really.'*

'I thought so,' said the doctor, and she frowned.

She grabbed the strange suit in one hand and my shoulder in the other. Her grip was surprisingly strong. 'It's just as I feared,' she whispered. '**Put the suit on, quickly.**'

'What's wrong?' I said, finding myself obeying and putting one leg inside the suit, and then the other. What on earth was I doing?

'**DRAGONS** can only digest food when their flame is on. Otherwise it quickly decomposes into a **gas** that inflates their lower stomachs. Unless it is burned off, it will get **very bad** for Carol.'

'What will happen?' I said.

The doctor turned away so Carol couldn't hear. 'First, the **burping** will get worse. At the moment it's just embarrassing. Soon it will become uncontrollable. Then she won't be able to get the gas out quickly enough and she'll start to *INFLATE* like a scaly balloon. Eventually she will just go . . .' Her voice trailed off.

'**POP!**' I whispered under my breath, and I looked across at poor Carol, who just then let out the most **enormous** ripping belch.

'**BUUUUUUUUUUURRRRRPGGGGGGGHHHHH!**

Oh dear! I'm SO, SO sorry!' she said. 'This is so **embarrassing!**'

I whispered to the doctor, 'You mean Carol might actually—'

'**Die.** Yes,' said the monster doctor blankly.

'As **dead** as a dodo jumping out of an upstairs window, I'm afraid. And the worst of it is the poor dear is so very young.'

'How long do dragons actually live for?' I asked.

'Oh, no more than a **thousand years,** give or take a century,' said the doctor. 'But Carol is barely out of her twenties, the *poor thing.* Judging from her teeth I'd say she was no more than **two hundred and eighty,** tops. She might well **live** for another seven or eight hundred years.'

She may as well have pulled a card from her sleeve marked:

and presented it to me.

Which is why five minutes later I was dressed in the doctor's **weird suit** and **helmet** (which she'd promised me was completely fireproof) and gazing up into Carol's **enormous** nostrils.

The doctor said, 'Stick out your tongue and say **AAAAAAH!**' (To Carol, not me.)

I watched as Carol's **enormous** jaws opened and her tongue unfurled like the ramp on a ferry. One end lay at my feet while the other disappeared into the dark and unwelcoming world of Carol's insides.

'*Good luck!*' said Carol as I stepped gingerly up and on to her tongue. I tiptoed carefully past her **razor-sharp** teeth. The doctor had already warned me about them – apparently dragon teeth are so sharp they can cut through anything, and they never, ever go blunt.

The leathery throat **narrowed** and **narrowed** until it became so tight I had to get down on my hands and knees. At first I crawled, then I writhed, then I squirmed like a **slug.**

The walkie talkie on my waist crackled into life. *'How's it going?'* asked the doctor.

'Oh, it's *lovely* in here,' I answered. 'It's like someone made an assault course out of meat.'

'That's the spirit!' said the doctor's voice. *'We'll make a monster doctor out of you yet, Nurse Ordinary. Just you wait until you have to do something really unpleasant – like empty an incontinent troll's bedpan. Ha! Anyway, you should be reaching Carol's forward combustion stomach about . . . NOW!'*

She was right. The grisly tube suddenly widened, and I flopped down into a pink space the size of a small spare bedroom, decorated by someone who had an obsession with princesses. Several other holes led off to other stomachs (apparently dragons have eight).

'Now look around and tell me what you see.'

The floor was a pool of **bubbly green goo** that **blobbed** and **popped** like a lava pit.

'This is **weird,**' I said. 'There's a Royal Mail

letterbox in here and a small family hatchback car.'

'*That sounds like a perfectly normal diet for a dragon,*' said the doctor's voice on the radio. '*But if you look up you should see something that looks a lot like a chandelier made of antlers.*'

I did.

'Excellent! Well, that's the dragon's pilot light. All you need to do now is use the blowtorch I gave you to light it.'

This wasn't so bad. Pretty easy even. I unhooked it from my belt and raised it to the pilot light. But just then the **gloopy** ground beneath my feet started to **bubble** and **rumble** like a geyser about to blow.

'Err ... **what's going on?**' I asked.

The doctor's voice crackled on the radio. She actually sounded a teensy bit **panicked.** *'Ah! Try to keep calm. Er ... keep VERY calm. Nothing to worry about at all. It's just that Carol is about to burp again,'* she said. *'So just one thing,'* she added. *'It's VERY important, but whatever you do –* **KZZZZZZTTT!** *–'* the radio cut out briefly – *'light the fire right now!'*

Just then one of the other tunnels behind me opened wide. **A hurricane of smelly air** blasted out and lifted me clean off my feet. Somehow I managed to grab hold of the car's wing mirrors and I hung there. I was suddenly in a wind tunnel designed to test **really bad breath.** The noise from the never-ending **'BELCH!'** was deafening. But somewhere, far, far away, I could hear the radio crackling. The doctor must be screaming at me to light the flame.

So I did.

I raised the **blowtorch** with my free hand and pressed the **start button.**

What followed was the **loudest BANG!** I have ever heard.

I REALLY HOPE I DON'T LAND ON THAT!

Chapter 10

I realized **(too late)** that the doctor's warning had obviously been, *'Whatever you do, DON'T light the fire now!'* Apparently relighting a dragon's pilot light while they are belching – like I had just done – turns its throat into a **giant** circus cannon. This is what is known in monster medicine circles as a V.S.I. (or **Very Stupid Idea.**)

Everything went a very bright shade of **orange*** for about half a second.

---

* If a paint company made that colour, they would probably call it Atomic Blast!

I suddenly felt like a **football** that was being kicked by someone wearing **jet-propelled** boots. This should have hurt quite a lot, but I didn't really notice. I was too busy being distracted by the fact that I was flying through the air.

'TRY AND AIM FOR SOMETHING SOFT,' yelled a voice from somewhere. I looked down and there, thirty metres below me, was the doctor. **'WAVE YOUR ARMS!'** she shouted. **'IT WILL SLOW YOUR FALL A BIT!'** This was probably good advice, but I didn't have much time to try it because I wasn't going to be flying for much longer. **Gravity** had suddenly noticed me and I was now falling – very quickly – **towards the ground**. More specifically, the bit of ground I was falling towards had old Miss Jorgensen's cottage on it.

This was **bad news.**

Falling from a great height is never good for the person doing the falling. But it looked as if it was going to be much worse for *Miss Jorgensen*. You see it wasn't just me that was falling from the sky. The entire contents of **CAROL'S** stomach had been blasted out along with me.

The small **hatchback car,** the **Royal Mail letterbox** (and assorted mail) and a large spray of **slimy green stomach gloop** were all heading in *Miss Jorgensen's* general direction.

Again, I should probably have been paying attention to the ground rushing up to meet me, but something *beautiful* was flying alongside me. It *glittered* as the **sunlight** caught its sharp and shiny edges. It was one of Carol's front teeth.

The **explosion** must have knocked it out. Just before I hit the ground I thought, *I really hope I don't land on that!*

I didn't.

Instead, I plopped down slap-bang in the middle of a huge heap of leaves that old Miss Jorgensen had raked together. **Hooray** for tidy gardeners! Miss Jorgensen was lucky too – amazingly, not one single thing hit her.

Unfortunately, her house wasn't quite so lucky.

The cloud of **sticky gooey stomach gloop** splashed down on her front lawn, but it blended right in on account of being so **disgustingly** green. The **Royal Mail letterbox** crashed into her cottage's roof, where it took a place as a second chimney. Smoke and burnt letters immediately began to pour out of the posting slot.

Miss Jorgensen (being a bit short-sighted) might not ever notice either of those two new additions, but eventually even she would spot the small hatchback car that had turned her upstairs back bedroom into a second-storey garage.

For now, though, she was far too busy banging on the cracked glass of my helmet with her pruning shears.

'Are you from the council?' she barked. 'I reported **a chip-pan fire** earlier and no one's called me back yet.' She pointed her trowel up towards the castle – without even looking at it. 'And now I can distinctly smell a barbecue. Does that very odd lady up there in the castle – you know, the one with bad teeth and that **terrible** skin condition – not realize how **dangerous** unattended fires can be? My cousin, **Colonel Slime-Wrangler,** came to a very sticky end on account of an unattended **fire.**

Well, that and the fact that he shouldn't have been climbing inside a **volcano—'**

Fearing that she might go on like this for a week or so, I seized my chance and stood up.

Brushing the leaves off my protective suit, I announced officiously, **'Ozzy Ordinary** at your service, ma'am. **Department of Annoying Neighbours.** As you can see from my protective clothing, we at the council are taking your concerns very **seriously** indeed. I'm heading over to the castle right now to get to the bottom of this. I suggest you go indoors immediately and stay there until I return. Our **scientists** have shown that the smoke from barbecues and chip pans can be very **harmful** to the elderly. **Don't go upstairs, though,'** I warned her sternly. 'The concentrations are higher in bedrooms – especially back bedrooms.'

She looked **shocked** and trotted obediently inside. I was heading out of the garden gate when I noticed Carol's tooth. It was embedded in the head of a **garden gnome.** I pulled it out, tucked it carefully under my arm and trudged back up the road towards the castle.

Carol was **pounding** down the hill towards me. The doctor was trying to catch up with her.

There was a clear gap in her front teeth where the **explosion** I'd caused had knocked her tooth out.

Oh dear.

A CUDDLE FROM
A DRAGON

Chapter 11

I stood there, shaking slightly and holding up the *glittering* dragon's tooth by its root.

'I'm **SO SORRY** about your tooth!' I said.

'My tooth?' Carol said, skidding to a halt with a cloud of fresh smoke billowing from her nostrils. She put one huge claw to her snout. 'I hadn't even noticed it was missing!' She **giggled.*** 'What **nonsense!** It's me that needs to *thank you!*' she gushed. *'You SAVED me!'*

And, to demonstrate, she blew an **enormous**

---

* A giggling dragon is a thing to see and is almost as cute as a tap-dancing **kraken.**

breath of **flame** up into
the air. Several roasted
seagulls dropped instantly
out of the sky.

Then, showing off a bit, she
puffed perfect smoke rings out through
the new gap in her teeth.

'*Ooh! I love it*,' she declared.
'Plus it will make me look **terrifying**
in my new publicity photos.'

She pushed the dragon tooth
back towards me. 'You keep it,'
she said. 'I've got **LOADS** more of them.' She
opened her jaws wide again just to remind me
about how many **razor-sharp** teeth a fully
grown dragon has.

Clue: it's a lot.

'Besides,' she continued, 'I'm sure you'll find
a use for it. The doctor was just telling me how
incredibly **dangerous** it was for you to help me.'

'She was?' I said. 'She never mentioned . . .'

The doctor stood with her hands behind her
back. She was prodding a freshly
roasted seagull with the toe of
one shoe and pretending
not to listen.

'Oh yes!' Carol continued. 'The doctor was
SO impressed that you even agreed to do such a
thing. She never thought you would, you know –
especially with the chance of **survival** being so
very low.' With that she bent down to *cuddle me*.
Now, I know she meant well, but a *cuddle* from
a dragon isn't much better than being **exploded**
out of its stomach. But, let's be **honest**, you don't
really refuse a *cuddle* from a dragon, do you?
Especially one that is purring.*

---

* A dragon's purr sounds like a cross between a very loud
tractor and a very quiet machine gun.

Carol would probably have squeezed me to death if the doctor hadn't interrupted. She was tapping her wristwatch in the universal gesture of *Hurry up!*

'Well, we really must be getting back to the surgery, **Nurse Ordinary,**' she said as she dragged me from Carol's clutches and steered me off towards the ambulance. '**Patients** waiting. **Dreadful** diseases. **Horrid** scabs. **Guts** hanging out all over the place. You know the sort of thing.' And she strode off towards the **ambulance.** I realized that she was actually going to leave without asking Carol for any payment.

No wonder she was so broke.

'**What about the bill?**' I hissed at her. But she just waved her free hand like the issue of money was to be dismissed as if it was nothing more than an **irritating** fly.

But Carol had heard me.

'Did you say bill?' she asked. 'How rude of me. I'll settle up with you now, if that's OK? Do you take cash?'

'**Absolutely,**' I said enthusiastically, breaking free of the doctor's grip.

'Wait a second,' Carol said as her tail rooted around inside the castle wall. 'Now, where did I put my purse? Ah! There it is! Right where I left it, by the fridge.' Her tail re-emerged, gripping a **large canvas bag** that chinked when she dropped it at my feet. 'I'm so sorry,' she said. 'I only keep a small amount of petty cash around the place these days. As soon as those **dreadful knights in armour** began stealing things at sword point, I moved most of my hoard to a **Swiss bank**. It's so much safer there.' She pulled open the top of the bag with a **claw** that was the size of a broadsword and said, 'I hope this will be enough?'

It was full to the brim with **huge** gold coins.

The doctor's mouth fell open and she began to protest. 'This is—'

But I cut her off.

'By a **strange** coincidence, this is exactly the right amount!' I said and quickly grabbed the bag. It took both hands to drag it to the ambulance (all the while nudging the open-mouthed doctor with my shoulder). '*Thank you*, **CAROL**. I'll send you a receipt by email. But we really must get away to another **emergency!** More **monsters** in **peril**.'

Carol waved goodbye. 'I understand,' she said, sniffing. 'You healers are so selfless! It must be **wonderful** to have a vocation – though I must say I do love burning armies and stealing gold,' she mused to herself.

I opened the ambulance's door and hissed, '**Quick! Get in!**' at the doctor.

'What are you up to?' said the doctor. 'There's a **fortune** in that bag.'

'Good grief! Morty told me you were useless with money, but I thought he was **exaggerating!** You heard Carol,' I said. 'This –' I kicked the bag and nearly broke my toe – 'is small change to her! She won't miss it at all, but it will stop your surgery falling down. That means you can help more sick and needy monsters, and, after getting me to crawl through a DRAGON'S INNARDS, get blown up and be shot out of her mouth, the least you can do is pay me.'

The doctor smiled. 'Oh that! That was just to make Carol trust you.'

'What?' I said.

'Well, would you let a completely unqualified stranger crawl around your insides?' she said. 'I had to make you look *good*. You were never in any real **danger.** The **worst** that could have happened is you might have lost a limb or two. You could just grow them back –' She stopped, looking puzzled. She'd noticed the strange face I was making. *'You're not going to tell me you can't grow limbs back, are you?'* she said.

I nodded.

'Smell colours?' she asked.

I shook my head.

'Fold paper with your tongue?'

'Nope.'

'Ah, that's **awkward,**' she said. 'I'd better apologize, then. But, if it's any consolation, you clearly have a gift for **monster medicine.**

Plus, you're *lucky* – or very hard to kill – both of which are **jolly helpful** in our line of business. Though if we're going to work together again, I really think we need to sit down and have a chat about what **human beings** can and can't do.'

She turned the key in the ignition and the ambulance roared into life. The engine vibrations made the large bag of gold coins jingle pleasantly at my feet.

'Bruce!' the doctor called, and the little bat stirred within his jar. He unfurled his wings, yawned and the **LED** screen lit up.

YAWN.
I WAS HAVING A LOVELY NAP!
WHERE DO YOU WANT TO GO NOW?

'Sorry, my little friend,' said the doctor. *'Please take us home.'*

'OPEN THIS DOOR AT ONCE!'

Chapter 12

The journey back wasn't any better than it had been on the way out, but at least it was a little more peaceful. The **BAT-NAV** took us along a barely used stretch of the **Great Wall of China** and

then found a shortcut through the **reading room** of the Little Bidlington community library. (We were very quiet and I don't think anyone noticed us.)

After a few minutes, the ambulance gave a **stomach-lurching jolt,** and we were suddenly trundling back down Lovecraft Avenue. Bruce squeaked and his **LED** screen lit up.

IN 100 METRES YOU WILL
HAVE REACHED YOUR DESTINATION.

Then a tiny set of dark blinds dropped down inside the jar.

I'M GOING TO BED NOW.

We were back. **Safe at last!** (Well, safe-ish, anyway.) But as the ambulance approached the surgery I could see a large van blocking the drive to number eleven.

The doctor sighed. *'Now what?'* she said, and jumped out. I followed close behind.

Big letters across the side of the van **(huge letters,** in fact) proudly proclaimed:

BERTRAND BEHEMOTH
BUILDING SERVICES

NO JOB TOO BIG
NO CLIENT TOO STRANGE

CASH ONLY DUE TO
NON-PAYMENT OF BILLS

A small crowd, of what I assumed were the surgery's patients, was waiting outside the front door. We squeezed past a **creature** the size of a **sofa** that looked like a cross between a **caterpillar** and a **centipede.** Twenty-three of its fifty pairs of legs were in plaster.

'What's going on, **Doc?**' the thing said. 'I need to get my casts off today!'

'I don't know, Mrs Millicent. But don't you **worry** about it. I'll soon get to the bottom of this,' the doctor said.

The rest of the patients made way for us. They were an **odd-looking** group. There was an aged (and badly balding) WEREWOLF, a **swamp-lizard** thing with webbed feet and a frilly head crest and some-thing else that looked for all the world like a collection of **animated** dustbins strung together with vacuum-cleaner hose. The only ones I recognized were the man and his daughter from earlier. They were back, although this time her head was on upside down. (I didn't ask.)

Then a familiar voice cried, *'Hello, Nurse Ordinary!'* But when I turned to look there was no one there. *'Down here!'* the voice announced, and I looked down into the friendly face of **Morty Mort.** His head was looking up at me from where it was tucked beneath his own arm.

'Don't tell me,' I said. **'FOOTBALL.'**

'I know,' he groaned. 'The doctor warned me, but what am I supposed to do? These stitches just can't cope with the **athletic lifestyle** choices of a **modern zombie.'**

By now the **doctor** had reached the front of the queue. There was an **enormous creature** heaving on the door handle of the surgery. It looked like an **elephant,** but one that had been created by a committee who thought the original elephant design wasn't **big** or **strong** enough. Its legs were the size of the columns of the Parthenon, and it wore a pair of workman's overalls that must have been made by a **circus-tent** manufacturer.

'Bert! What are you doing here?' the doctor asked with **surprise.** This was her former builder.

Bert saw the doctor and frowned. *'What does it look like, Doc? I'm trying to get in –* just like everyone else. I only popped by to see Delores and try to get paid. As you well know, I'm still waiting for payment on that **swamp-spa** treatment room I built for you.'

He pointed up at a **strange** extension that was leaking **foul-smelling** mud all down one wall. 'But even I can't get in. And, believe me, I have tried!' It was true. There were broken builders' tools all over the floor at this **giant's** feet. 'What on earth are you playing at, Doc?'

'**Nonsense!**' said the doctor. 'That door is never locked. We are never closed to sickly monsters.' She heaved Bert to one side and grabbed the door handle herself, **jiggled it, pulled it** and **tugged on it.** 'It's **LOCKED!**' she said in an outraged voice and hammered angrily on the door. '**DELORES!** Open this door at once!' she yelled. 'What is the meaning of this?'

Delores's unmistakable voice came from inside. '**DON'T YOU GO YELLING AT ME!**' she bellowed. 'It's not MY fault! It's that blobby Bob chap. He started **sneezing** just after you left and couldn't stop. He turned into a **snot-volcano.** I reckon he must have been allergic to those tablets you gave him.'

'I knew it!' I blurted out **unwisely.** 'They were **monster** aspirin! But Bob's a **THING.**' The doctor looked **horrified.**

'What have I done?' she said. 'How could I

make such a stupid mistake?

I must be getting too old for this.'

But Delores hadn't finished **moaning** yet. 'Of course we ran out of tissues, and then he started getting $snot$ absolutely everywhere.

I've never seen anything like it. It's on the doors, the windows, all over my glass partition. He's only gone and gummed up the **WHOLE surgery!'**

A second voice, much quieter than the first, piped up. **'I vewwy sowwy for being tho much twubble,'** said Bob. 'I shub hab warned you about by snot. I can't seeb to stob –'

Something **unpleasant** went **SPLAT!** on the inside of the door.

'**OH LORD!**' cried Delores. 'There he goes again! The **whole place** is **disgusting!** And I can tell you for a fact that I am not going to be cleaning it up. Oh dearie me, no!'

'A-A-A-A-ACHOOOOOOO!'

'Delores?' asked the doctor, who was growing increasingly annoyed. 'What on **EARTH** has Bob's snot got to do with the door not opening?'

'**I AM TRYING TO TELL YOU!**' Delores yelled back. 'His snot goes **hard** when it dries.'

'Of course it does,' said the **doctor,** looking confused. 'It's one of nature's many glories.'

'**NO! I mean REALLY hard!**' answered Delores. 'As **hard as concrete.** And the door is blocked by it.'

'Actually, it's much, much harder than concrete,' corrected Bert the builder. 'I've never seen anything like it, Doc. I've tried to cut it with my pickaxe, angle grinder and electric saw. **Nothing makes a dent in it.**'

'All right, everyone,' announced the doctor. 'Don't worry. I've got something in the ambulance that will open any door – even one coated in concrete snot.' She took my arm. **'Nurse Ordinary,** a hand, *if you please.*' And she flung open the back door of the ambulance.

The inside was full of equipment that would have looked more at home in **Bert the builder's van** than in an ambulance. There were picks, shovels, spades, jackhammers and even a small cement mixer. Three heavily padded metal drums were labelled **ACID – not to be drunk neat.** There was even something at the back that looked like (but surely couldn't be) a ship's cannon. The doctor slapped the top of a flat wooden box.

'Give me a hand with this,' she said.

'What is it?' I asked.

'Something that will definitely open that door,' she said, smiling. As we dragged it out of the ambulance, I read the stencilled letters on the side.

CAUTION
HIGH EXPLOSIVES
HANDLE WITH CARE

'IT'S EXTREMELY SHARP...'

Chapter 13

'Err . . . **explosives?**' I said. 'Is that wise?'

'What?' asked the doc, noticing me looking with horror at the label. She **laughed.** 'Oh! I see why you're worried. There are no explosives in here any more. I think I used the last of those when the Collossus of Agrivar accidentally sat down in a sinkhole and got his bottom stuck.' Then she whispered, 'It's **amazing** what eighty-five kilos of TNT will budge!'

She lifted the lid to reveal . . .

. . . a **chainsaw.**

But what a **chainsaw!** It had an engine **powerful** enough for a drag racer, and teeth so

big they would give a **great white shark** denture
envy.

'It's a **SNODGRASS 4400-RS**,' the doctor said
proudly. Then in response to my blank look she
explained, 'It is the finest **monster toenail and
horn trimmer.** Everyone knows the hardest
substance in the universe is a crusty toenail –'

that made **sense** – 'well, now **imagine** how hard a giant's are to cut! This thing will slice through them like a **red-hot** axe through butter. No snot glue is going to stop it. **STAND ASIDE!**' she shouted, and she grabbed hold of the starter cord to fire up the trimmer.

But Bert suddenly looked terrified! **'NO, NO, NO!'** he cried and snatched it from the doctor's hands. 'You can't go starting that contraption **HERE!** The vibration will bring the building down on our heads! I tried using my angle grinder earlier and the whole upper storey started shaking so **badly** that a block of stone landed on my helmet.'

He pointed to where a yellow builder's helmet lay on the floor. It had a **dent** in it the size of a cereal bowl.

'Are you all right?' I asked.

'Oh, don't you worry!' Bert laughed. 'My skull is harder than any **concrete block.** I only wear the helmet in case of an **unexpected** health-and-safety inspection – and to look a bit more professional. I've told the doc hundreds of times that this place is about as well-built as **the first little piggy's straw house.'** He turned to me and added, 'Which, I might add, I strongly warned **Percival Piggy** against. I mean, who on earth builds a house out of straw? **"You need brick!"** I told him. "Like your sensible sister, Penelope."'

The doctor put the toenail trimmer back into its box. 'Well, what are we supposed to do?' she asked.

Surely she wasn't **out of ideas?**

Bert the builder shook his head in the **universal** gesture of people about to give very expensive advice. 'There's nothing for it but to take the surgery down brick by brick. There's nothing that can cut through that **snot.**'

Something about the words 'cut through' made me stop and think. I pulled the dragon tooth out of my pocket. Carol had said that it was very sharp.

'What's that?' said Bert.

'By my *grandmother's* **furry green beard!'** cried the doctor. Her jaw was hanging open. 'What on earth are you doing with that?'

'Carol gave it to me,' I said.

The doctor held out her hand. 'May I?' she asked, and she took the **dragon tooth** from me very gently.

'Be careful!' I said. 'Carol said it's **EXTREMELY** sharp.'

The doctor snorted. 'I should say so. Back when I was in school, they used to make swords for kings out of these. A **dragon's tooth sword** can cut through anything, you know. Watch.' And she began to cut around the front door. The tooth didn't slow whether it was cutting wood, the metal hinge, brick,

or even **Bob's indestructible snot**. Nothing could stop it. When she'd cut all around it, the doctor stepped back, tapped the door gently with one finger and watched it fall inwards like a felled tree. *'Everyone! Please wait out here,'* she said to her patients and stepped inside.

Bert and I followed.

'AH! TO BE
SO YOUNG AGAIN!'

Chapter 14

'**W**ill somebody **PLEASE** get me out of here?'
hissed Delores from behind the screen of
her receptionist's booth. The glass was covered
with hardened gunky goo.

'I need the loo!' she announced. She did not
look happy at all, and her mood didn't even
improve after the doctor used the dragon tooth to
cut her free. '**RIGHT!**' she said, as she gathered
up three handbags, a pile of magazines, her
half-finished knitting and a packet of **Jammy
Dodgers.** 'That's it! I'm off! And I'm taking
the rest of the week off as well. You can clean
this mess up yourselves. And don't even think

of calling me until you've got rid of **Mr Snot Factory** over there –' she pointed one angrily quivering **tentacle** at **Bob,** who flinched – 'and made this place **safe** for decent hard-working monsters!' She shimmied angrily out of the door.

'**I'm EBBER so sowwy,**' sniffed Bob. He was **oozing** over the edges of a couple of chairs in the waiting room. He seemed unaffected by the glue. 'Oh, it doesthn't sthick to be for sthobe reason. I sthposthe I bust be lucky,' he said.

'Well, will you look at that?' said **Bert the builder.** He was staring in awe at the ceiling. The doc and I both looked up, but it was just the same crumbly ceiling it had been earlier, except now it was covered in a film of **Bob's rock-hard glue.**

'What?' said the doc. 'It's the same **horrible** ceiling you said you couldn't fix last week.'

'Not exactly,' said Bert. 'That ceiling was ready to fall down. But now look at it.' He punched it hard with his fist. **'Rock hard!'** He turned to Bob. 'Here, mate! Have you got any more of this gooey stuff?'

Bob laughed weakly. **'More? I nebber sthop making it! That's the pwoblem.'** And as if to emphasize the point, he sneezed again. **'A-A-A-A-A-AAAAAACCHHHHOOOOOOOOOOOO!!'**

It splattered against the wall by Bert.

'I'm tho sowwy!' Bob said for the hundredth time. But Bert just smiled, whipped out a trowel and scraped the **sloppy goo** off the wall.

BERT AND BOB'S BUILDERS

'Never you mind that, mate.' Bert laughed.
Then he went and fetched a bucket from his van.
He handed it to Bob and said, 'Just make sure
the next time you feel like **sneezing,** you do it in
there. If we can get that stuff into a tube before it
goes hard, it will be a **GOLD MINE,** Bob!' He put
one **enormous** arm round Bob's shoulders (or
where Bob's shoulders would have been, if he'd
had any).

'It's the **best** glue, mortar and cement I've ever seen. How do you fancy working with me? Come on out to my van and we'll have a quick chat. How does **BERT AND BOB'S BUILDERS** sound to you? We'll have to think of a name for your **snot**, though. Maybe—'

'**Bert! Wait!**' the doctor interrupted. 'How much to hire you and your new business partner to fix this place up?'

'Sorry, Doc,' said Bert as he and Bob headed for the door. 'I like you, I really do, but I'm not a charity. From now on it's strictly a case of no cash – no building.'

'**Hmm ... I see,**' said the **doctor** as she pulled out a handful of very large (and extremely **shiny**) gold coins from her pocket and let them **jingle** and **clatter** to the floor at Bert's feet.

The look on his face changed instantly. 'Right, then!' he said. 'I'll get my tools from the van! Bob, you get filling that bucket with bogey cement. I'll be back in a jiffy.'

The doctor and I followed Bert outside.

'I'm very sorry, everyone,' the doctor announced to the crowd of waiting patients, 'but the surgery will be **closed** for a couple of days due to –' another large block of stone **crashed** to the ground outside – 'structural repairs. We'll be reopening on Thursday.'

After a few **groans,** the patients began to drift away.

Morty waved to me. His head under his arm called out, 'See you later, **Nurse!**'

But right then an idea popped into my own head. I called out, **'Morty, wait!'** and grabbed the sample of Bob's snot I'd taken earlier.

'Can I try something?' I asked the monster doctor.

She seemed to read my mind, smiled and nodded agreement.

'Hold still,' I told Morty, and I poured the **glue** on to his **neck hole.** Then I gently took his head and stuck it back where it was supposed to be (giving it a strong *squeeze* to secure it and lashing it in place with bandages).

'There,' I said. 'You must promise to keep that perfectly still for at least an hour. **No football,** *no dancing* and **no boxing** for a whole day until it sets solid. Then you should never need **STITCHES** ever again!'

'**Wow!**' said Morty. '**You're a magician!**' He turned (very slowly and carefully) to the doctor. 'You should give **Ozzy** a go as your nurse, Doc. He's a **natural healer**,' he said.

'It is strange that Morty should say that,' the doctor said to me, 'I was thinking the very same thing. You see, you remind me of myself – when I was your age. Tell me, what are you? A hundred, a hundred and fifty years old? Ah! To be so **young** again!'

'Not quite,' I said.

'Even more **remarkable**,' she said. 'Well, you certainly have an **old-looking head** on your shoulders.' She held out her hand. 'Welcome to the world of **monster medicine.** Can I count on your help with Thursday night's **special** clinic? I'm sure you'd enjoy it.'

'I'd love to,' I said. 'What kind of clinic is it?'

The doctor smiled.

It was that huge smile that showed her rows and rows of tiny teeth.

'Vampire dentistry,' she said.

THE END

GLOSSARY

Baby sister: A small bag of human flesh filled with unpleasant noises and horrendous smells. Also comes in baby brother shape.

Basilisk: A charming and delightful monster whose gaze can, unfortunately, cause instant death. (Interestingly, a similar phenomenon can also be observed in human mothers.)

Blowtorch: A small tool for producing portable fire. Very popular since the use of hand-held baby dragons was banned for being too cruel. (Even though the draglings themselves insisted they enjoyed it.)

Cannonball: A ball of solid iron delivered to someone at very high speed. Definitely much more fun to send than receive.

Dead Rovers: A zombie football team currently playing in the Monster League (Brain-Dead Division). The statistics for their most recent season are as follows:

Played: 12
Lost: 12
Goals for: 0
Goals against: 7286

(They currently hold the record for the most injury time recorded in a single season.)

Gabble's disease: A deadly virus that causes the victim to turn blue (and then all the colours of the rainbow in random order). The patient then begins to talk non-stop nonsense until they die of starvation or land a job as a radio phone-in host.

Garden gnome: A disgraced former branch of the monster community. They were all convicted of crimes against fashion and condemned to be turned into stone. For some reason, humans put their remains in their gardens.

Gorgonzola: A substance scraped from the spaces between the toes of trolls. This is then pressed into blocks and sold as speciality cheese to humans with defective noses.

Jammy dodger: A biscuit that is reckoned, by many monsters, to be one of the top three greatest achievements of human beings. The other two being derelict buildings and the invention of the wardrobe.

Knights in armour: Strange humans who like to dress up in tin cans and hit each other over the head with sharpened bits of metal. It's a bit like bell-ringing, but you're standing inside the bell.

Kraken: A species of giant octopus that, contrary to human myth, is extremely friendly. They enjoy tap-dancing, juggling and all-in wrestling. Unfortunately this has led to some very awkward misunderstandings with human ships over the years.

Latin: An ancient human language that was spoken by the Romans when they weren't too busy having baths. It's now only used by sentimental monsters, and some of the more bizarre human species of teachers and lawyers.

Oxen: What a cow would look like if it was drawn by a short-sighted cow.

Rapid Rabid Rabbit Racing: This is the world's bestselling computer game, despite the fact that it is banned in every single country. In the game, Rabbie Rabbit has rabies and you have to get him to hospital before pest control can catch him.

The Official World GLOOP Spectrum: A measurement system that was introduced to guard against cheap imports of gloop, goo and slime from some of the more unscrupulous dimensions.

Reverse-wibble: An unpleasantly dizzy manoeuver, very similar to the more common reverse-flollop. An expert can spot the difference between the two purely from the colour of the vomit produced afterwards.

Teachers: A primeval form of life that, way back in the mists of time, split from the common ancestor of monsters and humans.

Vampire dentistry: Exactly like normal dentistry, but with larger, sharper teeth. Vampire dentistry is the only branch of the profession where the dentist is more scared than the patient.

Wales: A country in the UK lying at an altitude somewhere between +1085m above and −3m below sea level. Officially the seventeenth dampest spot on earth.

Wodon Wulf-tree: Wodon was an unbending tyrant who led the forest of Wodondoor against the peaceful people of Pangolin. (Apparently they had said something rude about one of his shrubs.) Wodon was finally stopped − burnt − by Carol the Combustor, an up-and-coming young dragon with a very promising future in the burning armies business.

Turn the page to read an exclusive extract from

Ozzy and the doctor's next hilarious adventure,

Monster Doctor: Beastly Breakout

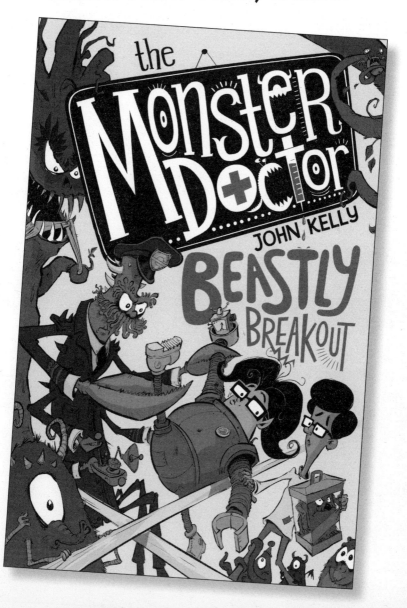

A DOG AT EACH END

Chapter 1

I was heading down the street towards the monster doctor's surgery when I saw **Morty the zombie walking a zombie dog.** I'd just rounded the corner where the human world turns into the monster world. You might know the place? It's just past the unicycle repair shop, but before **VLAD THE VAMPIRE'S** all-night convenience store.

'Good morning, **Morty!**' I called out.

'Morning, **Ozzy!**' wheezed **Morty.**

To my surprise, he looked quite smart. Most of his **limbs** were intact, and his **eyeballs** and **ears** were all where they were supposed to be. Even his head had stayed where I'd glued it back on last week, and, amazingly, nothing else had fallen off in the meantime.

His dog, on the other hand, was a **scruffy** black and white thing.

'What's his name?' I asked.

'**Tug**,' Morty replied.

Tug grinned up at me with a mouth as gappy as Stonehenge. He seemed happy enough – considering that he was a zombie dog. But I noticed that his nose was missing.

'Your dog's got **no nose**,' I said.

Morty grinned. 'That depends on which end you're looking at,' he said.

The other end of the dog – the end where it's traditional to have a bottom – had a completely **different dog's head**. Unlike Tug, this one looked pretty good. He had short black hair, a mouth full of teeth and a nice shiny nose.

'Isn't it a problem that your dog – or dogs – have **no bottom** between them?' I asked.

'Not really,' Morty said. 'It actually saves me a small fortune in poo bags. Which isn't to be sniffed at.'

(Unless you were a **zombie dog** with no nose, of course.)

'What's this one's name?' I asked.

'She's called **'War!'** Morty sniggered. **'Tug! War! Geddit?'** And he laughed until both his ears dropped off.

I picked them up and popped them in my pocket.

'Come on, Morty,' I said. 'I'll walk you to the surgery and **STITCH** these back on for you.'

'Speak up, Ozzy!' Morty said. 'I seem to have gone a bit deaf all of a sudden!' So I asked him again in a **louder** voice.

'That's very kind,' he said, 'but I was heading there anyway. War's been a bit poorly since she ate two postman's legs last week!'

I wasn't sure whether the legs were from more than one postman. And I forgot to ask later — what with everything that happened.

We had just crossed the road by **The Battered Squid** chippy and passed beneath the new street sign that stated

when a question occurred to me.

'Shouldn't you should be taking **Tug-o-War** to a monster vet?' But Morty just shook his head and pointed to the logo on my **MONSTER DOCTOR TRAINEE** T-shirt. It said **'CURIA OMNIA'** which is Latin for **'HEAL ANYTHING'** and is the motto of the Monster Doctors Organisation.

Morty was right, of course. The distinction between **monsters** and **things*** and their pets is a

*Monsters and things are very different.

Monsters are born weird.

Things are made weird by events.

All 'thing' types can be classified by a simple letter code. For example, Morty is a 'D-T' which stands for Dead-Thing.

For more about **Monsters** and **Things** see Ogbert & Nish's Monster Maladies or the more definitive reference book, *10,001 Interesting things about Things.*

bit pointless when either of them might have two hundred and seven tentacles.

We rounded the corner into 𝒧𝓸𝓿𝓮𝓬𝓻𝓪𝒻𝓽 𝒜𝓿𝓮𝓷𝓾𝓮 and there, dead ahead, was the monster doctor's surgery.

The surgery stands (or rather **leans**) somewhere between **five** and **seven** storeys high. When I'd first seen it at the beginning of the school holidays, large bits of it had been regularly falling off. This was due to both the doctor's funding issues (i.e. total lack of) and a nasty leak from the third storey **swamp-creature treatment suite.**

But after the doctor and I had cured the life-threatening indigestion of an enormous **DRAGON** called Carol, which had involved her swallowing me and then explosively vomiting me out between her razor sharp jaws, Carol had given us a great big bag of gold coins as a thank you. So the doctor could now afford the urgent repairs.

Morty and I paused before the surgery's now familiar brass plaque.

---

10 Lovecraft Avenue
Annie von Sichertall VIII
M.D.F.R.S.C.D.
Fully qualified monster physician & surgeon
Anything treated
(No biting allowed within these premises)

'C'mon Morty,' I said.

I was looking forward to the nice simple job of

stitching a zombie's ears back on, and was just
thinking of the cup of tea and a biscuit I'd have
afterwards, when the most awful noise erupted
from inside the surgery.

TO BE CONTINUED . . .

Acknowledgements

None of the complete nonsense you have just read would have been possible without the inspiration and help of the following people.

My wife Cathy for being so delightfully wonderful and weird in equal measures. Jodie and Emily at United Agents for believing in me – even when I didn't anymore. Macmillan for taking the risk of actually spending good money on the ramblings of a bearded old lunatic. Lucy, Cate, Rachel, Sue, Amanda, and everyone at Macmillan for being such an utter joy to work with.

ABOUT THE AUTHOR

John Kelly is the author and
illustrator of picture books such
as *The Beastly Pirates* and *Fixer*,
the author of picture books *Can I Join
Your Club* and *Hibernation Hotel*, and
the illustrator of fiction series such
as *Ivy Pocket* and *Araminta Spook*.
He has twice been shortlisted for the
Kate Greenaway prize, with *Scoop!*
and *Guess Who's Coming for Dinner*.
Monster Doctor is his first author-
illustrator middle-grade fiction.